First published 1986 by Walker Books Ltd
87 Vauxhall Walk, London SE11 5HJ
This edition published 2010
2 4 6 8 10 9 7 5 3 1
© 1986 Michelle Cartlidge
The right of Michelle Cartlidge to be identified as author/illustrator of this work
has been asserted by her in accordance with the Copyright, Designs and Patents Act 1988
Printed in China
British Library Cataloguing in Publication Data:
a catalogue record for this book is available from the British Library
978-1-4063-3316-9
www.walker.co.uk

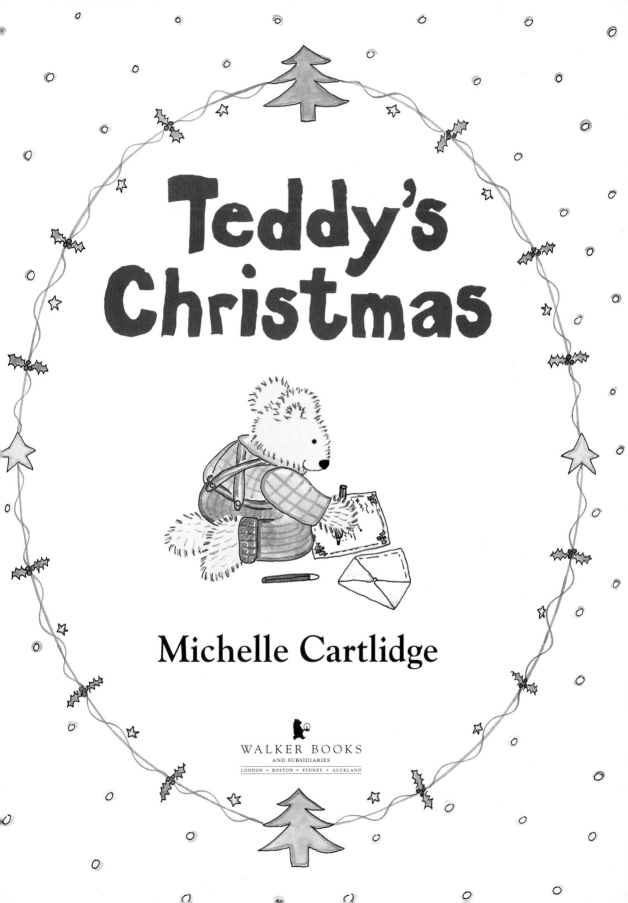

Teddy's Christmas

Michelle Cartlidge

WALKER BOOKS
AND SUBSIDIARIES
LONDON · BOSTON · SYDNEY · AUCKLAND

Teddy and his mummy went into town to do their Christmas shopping.
'I've got my letter for Father Christmas tucked safely in my pocket,' said Teddy.

There were carol singers outside
the toyshop.

'Look at all the lovely toys! Can we
go inside, Mummy?' asked Teddy.

Inside the shop, everyone was busy buying presents.

'Look at that panda, Mummy,' said Teddy.

'Perhaps Father Christmas will bring you one,' said Mummy.

Mummy bought some wrapping paper.
'Oh, Teddy, we have enough now.
Let's put that paper back and go
and see Father Christmas.'

'Oh good!' said Teddy. 'I can give
him my letter.'

'Hello, Father Christmas,' said Teddy.
'I've brought my Christmas list for you.
Please can I have a train set,
a big panda, a pot of honey and
a ball for my cat?'

'I'll see what I can do,' said
Father Christmas.

'I think we need a rest now,' Mummy said. 'Let's have a special Christmas tea.'

'Please can I have a cake with a cherry on?' asked Teddy.

Teddy and his mummy took all their presents home. Daddy met them at the gate.

'Oh look, Daddy! You've put the Christmas tree up. Can we decorate it now?' asked Teddy.

Teddy and the cat played with the
decorations.

'Please pass me the tinsel, Teddy,'
said Mummy.

'Look, Mummy! Our naughty cat has
seen the Christmas mouse sitting on
top of the tree,' said Teddy.

'Time for bed now,' Daddy said.
'We'll hang your Christmas stocking
at the end of your bed. I'll read you
a bedtime story.'

'Will you read me the one about
Father Christmas, please?' asked Teddy.

'Merry Christmas, Teddy!'
said Mummy and Daddy and Gran
and Grandpa on Christmas Day.

'Come on,' Mummy said. 'Let's open
the presents now.'

'Look,' said Teddy, 'Father Christmas
remembered the big panda on my list!'

'Oooh, that smells good!'
said Daddy.
   'I'm really hungry,' said Teddy.
   'Well, there's lots and lots for
everyone,' Mummy said. 'And there's
a great big pudding as well.'

After lunch, Teddy and Daddy
made a snowman in the garden.
Then they had a snowball fight.
'I wish it could be Christmas
every day,' said Teddy.